A Time of
GOLDEN DRAGONS

Song Nan Zhang and Hao Yu Zhang

Illustrated by Song Nan Zhang

Tundra Books

Published in Canada by Tundra Books, *McClelland & Stewart Young Readers*,
481 University Avenue, Toronto, Ontario M5G 2E9

Published in the United States by Tundra Books of Northern New York,
P.O. Box 1030, Plattsburgh, New York 12901

Library of Congress Catalog Number: 00-131206

Canadian Cataloguing in Publication Data

Zhang, Song Nan, 1942-
   A time of golden dragons

ISBN 0-88776-506-8

1. Dragons – China – Juvenile literature. I. Zhang, Hao Yu. II. Title.

GR830.D7Z42 2000   j398.24'54   C00-930418-5

We acknowledge the support of the Canada Council for the Arts
and the Ontario Arts Council for our publishing program.

We acknowledge the financial support of the Government of Canada through
the Book Publishing Industry Development Program for our publishing activities.

Printed and bound in Hong Kong, China

1 2 3 4 5 6   05 04 03 02 01 00

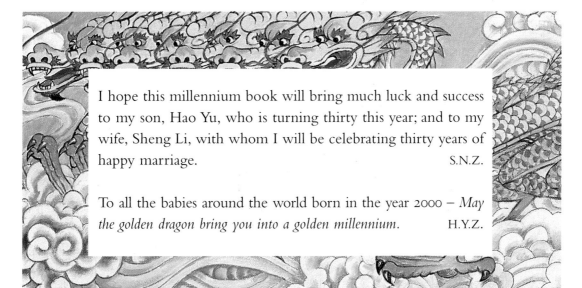

Before There Were Dragons

Long ago, when ancient people looked up at the sky, they saw how the sun, moon, and stars all changed. They saw the sun rise and set, and they gave names to day and night. They watched the moon's phases, and they called that passage a month. They gave names to the seasons to mark the time of cold and warmth. They named the years to mark the full cycle of seasons. With names, they brought order out of chaos.

In those days, animals were very powerful: human survival depended on the food and clothing they provided. Many peoples – the Chinese, the Egyptians, the Babylonians, the Africans, and the Native Americans – all used animal names to describe periods of time. The Chinese, however, looked beyond the animals around them when they chose names for time: they called on the name of the dragon.

The Chinese mark a cycle of twelve years, each named after a different significant animal. The spirits of people are believed to have the power, the character, and the temperament of the animal sign for the year in which they are born. In Chinese astrology, Dragon Years carry the greatest prestige. People who are born in Dragon Years are naturally gifted leaders. They are showered with good fortune.

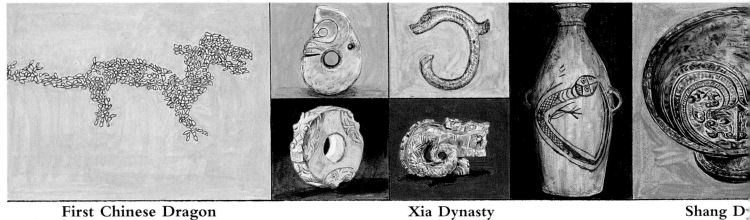

First Chinese Dragon
ca. 3600 B.C.E.

Xia Dynasty
ca. 21st century-ca. 16th century B.C.E.

Shang D
ca. 16th century-

Five Thousand Years of Chinese Dragons

Where Dragons Come From

Qing Dynasty
1644-1911 C.E.

Ming Dynasty
1368-1644 C.E.

Yuan Dynast
1279-1368 C.

Zhou Dynasty
ca. 1066–221 B.C.E.

B.C.E.

**Qin Dynasty
221–207 B.C.E.**

The godlike, mythical dragon most likely had an earthly origin. Historians think that the early dragon image was inspired by giant crocodiles. It is also possible that early humans lived at the same time as certain remnant species of dinosaurs.

The way dragons are depicted has changed from the earliest image found on shells. By around the 3rd century B.C.E., the Chinese finally settled on the dragon image we recognize today.

The image of the dragon is made up of the parts of several familiar animals. It is usually shown with a pair of deer antlers, a camel's head, a serpent's neck, a frog's belly, a fish's scales, a tiger's claws, a phantom's eyes, an eagle's nails, and an ox's ears. Perhaps each of these animals was worshipped as a tribal god by different groups of people who lived in the land that is now China. When these groups slowly merged to become one people, their animal symbols were blended into the image of the Chinese dragon.

**Han Dynasty
206 B.C.E.–220 C.E.**

**Period of Disunity
220–581 C.E.**

**Sui Dynasty
581–618 C.E.**

**Song Dynasty
960–1279 C.E.**

**Tang Dynasty
618–907 C.E.**

Dragons East and West

Chinese dragons have commonly been symbols of friendship and protection. They were thought of as gods who could fly to the highest skies and swim in the deepest seas. Dragons were also the loyal servants of the Sun God. With his son, the Sun God drove a fiery carriage drawn by dragons from the eastern horizon to the western horizon every day.

Dragons in Western stories are often evil and brutal. Only the bravest of the brave can conquer them.

The Emperor's Dragon

It is not surprising that the dragon became the symbol of absolute imperial power. The emperors who ruled China believed themselves to be the earthly reincarnations of dragons. Chinese emperors ruled from dragon thrones, lived in dragon-themed palaces, and dressed in silk robes heavily embroidered with dragons. Dragons were so powerful and prestigious that ordinary people were forbidden to use their image.

The Chinese believed that the dragon Pangu, the very first deity of China, separated the earth and sky, creating heaven and earth. His body transformed into mountains and rivers, and his spirits became the gods. These first gods divided up the universe so that each one controlled his own empire and one of the five elements.

The emperor of all emperors, known as the Central or Yellow Emperor, ruled the yellow earth. The Earth Spirit was his servant and the Yellow Dragon protected his court. Four other emperors controlled the four corners of the earth, and the four seasons.

The Southern or Fiery Emperor controlled fire and summer. The Spirit of Fire was his servant and the Fire Bird guarded his court.

The Eastern or Blue Emperor ruled spring. The Spirit of the Wood served him and the Blue Dragon protected his court.

The Western or White Emperor controlled autumn. His element was gold, and his court was guarded by the White Tiger.

The Northern Emperor presided over winter, and because the winter sky was always gloomy, he was known as the Black Emperor. He was served by the Water Spirit and guarded by the Black Beast.

All Chinese are descendants of one of these five heavenly emperors, and thus we are all the descendants of dragons.

Where Do Dragons Live?

Although they were imperial creatures, dragons were not confined to the emperor's palace. They were often associated with water. Early Chinese legends tell of dragons living in deep, remote mountain lakes or under the sea. These legends make sense if the first images of dragons were indeed based on giant crocodiles.

More stories of dragon kings spread to China from India as part of the Buddhist tradition. Buddhists believed that a great serpent god, or dragon king, ruled the oceans. As Buddhist influence grew in China about a thousand years ago, the image of dragons as rulers of the water became entwined with Chinese myths.

Among the myths were stories of dragon kings who lived in the water and ruled the four seas. Theirs was an entirely mythical underwater world, just as orderly as the one they had on the earth. In this water world, fish turned into laborers and merchants; shrimps and crabs became guards and warriors.

One of the greatest works of Chinese literature is the *Monkey King*. It is based on the true story of a Chinese monk who walked all the way to India in the 7th century. His travels were turned into an allegory that mingled ancient Chinese legends with the stories he heard in India. In one of them, the Monkey King visited the underwater kingdom of the Dragon King and grabbed its crown treasure – a huge iron bar that had been the ballast for the seas.

During the Ming Dynasty, many of the stories of dragon kings of the sea were written down and have been popular in China ever since.

Speaking Dragon

Throughout much of Chinese history, images of dragons were the exclusive domain of the emperors. But even emperors cannot stop ordinary people from thinking or speaking "dragon." Dragons were so important that they have crept into daily language.

For instance, it is believed that the Yellow River originated from heaven: the gods built a dragon gate at one of its highest points to prevent undeserving fish from accidentally entering heaven. Only those who fought the current and jumped over the incredible height of the gate could be turned into dragons and admitted to the heavenly court. Today, we say that someone who has overcome great obstacles has "jumped the dragon gate."

Reclining dragon:

A person of great talent who shirks his duty.

Dragon swirl:

A cyclone, tornado, or momentous event.

Dragon eye fruit:

Longan.

Dragon gate:

A great challenge.

Dragon Boat Race

Because dragons are so prominent in Chinese folklore, all our festivals involve them in one way or another. We celebrate with dragon dances and dragon lantern shows; we eat noodles that we call dragon whiskers.

One of the most popular festivities of the year, and the one with the longest history, is the dragon boat race. The first race took place in the early summer of 277 B.C.E. to commemorate the death of Qu Yuan, one of China's greatest poets.

In a moment of despair, Qu Yuan drowned himself in the Mi Luo River. The villagers rushed out in boats in a vain attempt to rescue him. To prevent the fish from disturbing his body, they tossed steamed rice cakes into the water.

Soon people throughout south China marked the day by organizing boat races. The boats were decorated with dragon heads on their bows, and became known as dragon boats. Nowadays, dragon boat races have become exciting international events. We no longer toss rice cakes into the river. The practice grew into the present custom of eating *tzungtzu*, delicious rice dumplings filled with ham or bean paste and wrapped in bamboo leaves.

Modern Dragons

The spirit of the dragon is everywhere in China. To bring some of its power and splendor to the places where we live, we have named thousands of sites throughout China after dragons. Plants, food, household items, toys, and even children are named after them.

Dragons have adapted to the modern world, appearing in movies and cartoons. Children and adults fly dragon kites, ride in dragon sleighs, and eat dragon buns.

Over thousands of years, the image of the dragon has changed from prehistoric totem to a symbol of absolute imperial power and, finally, to a symbol of the Chinese people.

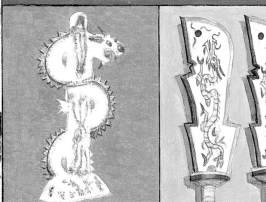

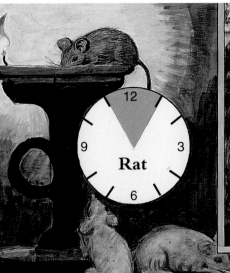

Dragon Time

The Chinese use the twelve animals to mark the passage of hours ea day, as well as the passage of years. Each day is divided into twelve equal time units called *shi*. And each unit has its own animal quality.

Rat — [Charm]
Hour: People are sound asleep, while rats forage for food
Year: Enterprising, but a bit stingy.

Ox — [Industry]
Hour: In the night stillness, oxen chew their cud.
Year: Dependable, persistent, and hardworking.

Tiger — [Courage]
Hour: In the darkest part of night, tigers are most ferocious and hungry.
Year: Tenacious and open-minded.

Rabbit — [Peace]
Hour: Just before sunrise, moon rabbits are the busiest.
Year: Soft-spoken and kind.

Dragon — [Fortune]
Hour: When the sun is not yet too hot, dragons bring mist or rain for crops.
Year: Authoritative, high-spirited, and powerful.

Snake — [Sagacity]
Hour: As the day is growing warm, reptiles venture out of their dens.
Year: Calm, stealthy, and analytical.

Tiger

Rabbit

Dragon

Horse [Fervor]
Hour: Horses have been fed by now and are running wild.
Year: Warmhearted, generous, and independent.

Ram [Artistry]
Hour: The afternoon is the best time to herd sheep on open pastures.
Year: Stylish and generous.

Monkey [Imagination]
Hour: After a day of foraging, it's playtime for monkeys.
Year: Competitive, coolheaded, and insatiable.

Rooster [Honesty]
Hour: The rooster sings as all the farm animals return to the barn.
Year: Fashionable, straightforward, and talkative.

Dog [Fidelity]
Hour: Darkness falls, and all may sleep – except the guard dogs.
Year: Truthful, fair, just, and adaptive.

Pig [Family]
Hour: Pigs are sound asleep; it is believed they gain the most weight during this Hour.
Year: Simple, kind, but gullible.

Snake

Ram

Horse

The Year of the Dragon

Not only does the Chinese calendar move through a twelve-year cycle of animal symbols, but it is affected by another cycle of about two years in length that moves through the five basic elements in this order: wood, fire, earth, metal (gold), and water. A Golden Dragon Year, which symbolizes the longing of people everywhere for happiness, prosperity, and peace, comes when the element Gold is paired up with the Dragon sign. This happens only once in every sixty years.

Of all the mystical signs or symbols, the Chinese are most fond of the Dragon. A Dragon Year is believed to bring much change and great good fortune.

The Chinese Dragon Year meets a Western Millennium Year every 3,000 years. The last time the Dragon knocked on a millennium door was in 1,000 B.C.E. The next Millennium Golden Dragon Year will come in 5,000 C.E.

By looking at this chart and moving through the cycle, you can identify the sign for anyone's year.

SIGN	DATE OF BIRTH	ELEMENT
Rat	February 2, 1984 to February 19, 1985	Wood
Ox	February 20, 1985 to February 8, 1986	Wood
Tiger	February 9, 1986 to January 28, 1987	Fire
Rabbit	January 29, 1987 to February 16, 1988	Fire
Dragon	February 17, 1988 to February 5, 1989	Earth
Snake	February 6, 1989 to January 26, 1990	Earth
Horse	January 27, 1990 to February 14, 1991	Metal
Sheep	February 15, 1991 to February 3, 1992	Metal
Monkey	February 4, 1992 to January 22, 1993	Water
Rooster	January 23, 1993 to February 9, 1994	Water
Dog	February 10, 1994 to January 30, 1995	Wood
Pig	January 31, 1995 to February 18, 1996	Wood
Rat	February 19, 1996 to February 6, 1997	Fire
Ox	February 7, 1997 to January 27, 1998	Fire
Tiger	January 28, 1998 to February 15, 1999	Earth
Rabbit	February 16, 1999 to February 4, 2000	Earth
Dragon	**February 5, 2000 to January 23, 2001**	**Metal (Gold)**
Snake	January 24, 2001 to February 11, 2002	Metal
Horse	February 12, 2002 to January 31, 2003	Water
Sheep	February 1, 2003 to January 21, 2004	Water
Monkey	January 22, 2004 to February 8, 2005	Wood
Rooster	February 9, 2005 to January 28, 2006	Wood
Dog	January 29, 2006 to February 17, 2007	Fire
Pig	February 18, 2007 to February 6, 2008	Fire

The words of a popular new Chinese song, written thousands of years after the first artist scratched a picture of a wondrous creature onto shells, tell us that the dragon still holds our imaginations and our hearts.

> Far away in the East, a river flows;
> People call it the Yellow River.
> Far away in the East, a dragon glows;
> People call it the China dragon.
> Reared and nurtured under its wings,
> Far and away we've traveled.
> Sons and daughters of dragons
> We shall always remain.